To Ginger Knowlton.

Many thanks for being in my corner.

I'm always happy to see your smiley faces ;) !

—G.C.L.

For Eda, Mary Anne, and Russ

—S.N.

Betsy Who Cried Wolf   Text copyright © 2002 by Gail Carson Levine

Illustrations copyright © 2002 by Scott Nash

Printed in Hong Kong. All rights reserved. www.harperchildrens.com

Library of Congress Cataloging-in-Publication Data   Levine, Gail Carson.   Betsy who cried wolf / by Gail Carson Levine ;
illustrated by Scott Nash   p.   cm. Summary: A serious young shepherd finds that there is more than one way to keep
a wolf from eating her sheep. ISBN 0-06-028763-2 — ISBN 0-06-028764-0 (lib. bdg.)   [1. Shepherds—Fiction.
2. Wolves—Fiction.] I. Nash, Scott, date, ill. II. Title.   PZ7.L578345 Be 2002   00-054032   [E]—dc21   CIP   AC

Typography by Carla Weise

1 2 3 4 5 6 7 8 9 10

❖

First Edition

BETSY
Who Cried Wolf

BAA!

Gail Carson Levine
Illustrated by Scott Nash

⬛ HarperCollins Publishers

n her eighth birthday,

Betsy took the Shepherds' Oath.

She was going to be the best

shepherd in Bray Valley history.

And any wolf who tried to eat

her sheep had better watch out!

That night, while Betsy slept in her bedroom above her mom's bakery, Zimmo howled on Rosenrise Mountain. *Ooo hoo hoooooo!* He was hungry. *Boo! Hoo! Hoo!* He was lonely. The sheep were always guarded, and he was the last wolf on the mountain.

He needed a Plan.

He thought. *Umm . . . Hmm . . . Umm . . .*

He howled. *Aii yii . . .*

Yii! He had it—a Plan to trick the shepherd and the farmers. It wouldn't make him less lonely, but he'd get to eat the sheep. He howled merrily. *Tralee traloo!*

Early the next morning, Betsy packed her lunch pail with two helpings of Mom's pies. Then she led the sheep up Rosenrise. When they got there, she scanned the slope to her left. No wolves. She scanned to her right. No wolves, but a ewe was trying to jump into the Soakenwetz River. Betsy drove her back and then scanned straight ahead. No wolves.

All right!

Hidden in a thicket halfway up the mountain, Zimmo watched Betsy. She looked tough, but he'd fool her anyway.

Betsy scanned to the left again.
Zimmo stepped out of the thicket.
Was it a wolf? Betsy reviewed
her Wolf Checklist.
Long snout? Check.
Bushy tail? Check.

BAA!

He's wearing a woolen muffler.

It *was* a wolf! Betsy blew her wolf whistle and cried, "Wolf!" exactly as she'd been taught in Shepherd School.

Every farmer in Bray pounded up to the pasture.

Zimmo slipped into his thicket and watched. Those farmers could scare an ordinary wolf, but not Zimmo, not a hungry wolf with a Plan.

"Where's the wolf?" Farmer Woolsey shouted.

Betsy pointed. "There!"

But the wolf had vanished.

Safe in his hiding place, Zimmo chuckled—and his stomach rumbled.

Farmer Woolsey scowled. "Are we going to lose the whole flock again, Betsy?" Long ago, Bray Valley had lost its sheep because of a mischievous shepherd. "Should we send you back to Shepherd School?" he thundered.

"No, sir! There was a wolf."

Farmer Woolsey just shook his head and started back to his fields. All the farmers shook their heads and followed him. None of them believed Betsy.

Zimmo almost felt sorry for Betsy. It wasn't her fault she
was up against a hungry, lonely wolf with a Plan.

Betsy went back to work.

Scan right. No wolves.   Scan left. No wolves.

Scan straight ahead. No wolves.

All right!

Time for lunch. Betsy reached into her lunch pail. She'd
protect the sheep, no matter what. She'd show those farmers.

Zimmo waited. Let her eat in peace, he thought. He scratched a flea and then ate it. Some lunch for a wolf!

Betsy finished her rhubarb pie. Scan right.

THAT WOLF AGAIN!!

Zimmo felt bad about tricking Betsy, so he howled, *Ooo eee eee!*

She had him now! She blew her whistle. She hollered, "Wolf! Wolf!"

When she turned to look for the farmers, Zimmo tiptoed away,

feeling like a skunk. But he had to follow the Plan. A wolf had to eat!

Only half as many farmers came this time. Not one saw even a hair

of a wolf. Farmer Woolsey took away Betsy's whistle and sent her back

to Shepherd School.

The next morning, Farmer Woolsey let Betsy have the flock again.

But he said it was her last chance.

When she reached the pasture, she scanned right. No wolves.

She scanned left.

THAT WOLF AGAIN!

But this time he was—

BARING HIS FANGS!

GALLOPING!! DOWN THE MOUNTAIN!!! TOWARD THE SHEEP!!!!

Betsy blew her whistle. She cried wolf. "Wolf! Wolf!!" She turned to look down the slope.

Nobody was coming!

She had to stop the wolf herself!

Betsy spun around to watch him. Her foot knocked into her lunch pail, and her pie helpings tumbled out.

Zimmo stopped short and sniffed. *Yumm!* The sheep just smelled like wool, but those pies smelled *DEElicious.* He took a step toward them.

My, he was skinny, Betsy thought. Poor wolf, he was starving. Still, she had a job to do! She picked up her tin plate of shepherd's pie to hurl at him.

Zimmo sat on his haunches and howled. A tear trickled down his cheek.

Betsy lowered her arm. So far he hadn't hurt the sheep.
If he wanted her lunch, he could have it.

She put the plate down and stepped back. "Help yourself."

Yumm! Zimmo rushed at the two big helpings of pie.

Betsy watched. For a second, she thought about petting him.
But a shepherd couldn't pet a wolf!

Zimmo wolfed down Betsy's lunch and licked the plate clean.

He felt much better now, so he wagged his tail and trotted away.

Halfway up Rosenrise, Zimmo hid behind a tree and watched Betsy.

A ewe had gotten stuck to a bramble bush, and she was pulling the brambles out one by one. What a fine shepherd she was!

But—uh-oh! Those lambs over there were too close to the cliff.

Look, shepherd! Look!

But she was too busy, and the lambs—

BAAAA!

Zimmo had to save them! He bounded down the mountain, growling and snarling.

Betsy whirled around.

That wolf!

Charging at the sheep!

And she didn't have any more lunch to give him!

She picked up a stone.

But she didn't throw it, because . . .

He was chasing the lambs back to the flock! He was herding them!

He was great at it, too!

For the rest of the day, Zimmo helped Betsy with the herding. When the sheep didn't need them, Betsy petted Zimmo and he taught her to howl. Then they sang together. *Tralaa tralee. Ha ha haloo.*

That night Betsy took Zimmo home to eat chicken pot pie and sleep in her room over her mom's bakery. In the morning, Farmer Woolsey and the other farmers apologized to Betsy.

Next, Zimmo howled the Shepherd's Oath. *Kee eee eep! Shee eee eep! Saay aay aafe!*

From then on, Betsy and Zimmo herded together and ate Mom's pies together, the two shepherds of Bray.